The Last Christmas Present

The Last Christmas Present

by Matt Novak

It was Christmas Eve at the North Pole.

Everyone was busy, especially Irwin.

The others were always telling him what to do.

After Santa had gone,

Irwin discovered something.

The big elves said,

But Irwin could not sleep.

So he set out to deliver the present himself.

He encountered many dangers.

Crack...

Uh-Oh.

But finally he arrived

and found the right street

and the right house.

He sneaked inside,

and Santa let him put the present under the tree

all by himself.

Then they flew home,

where Santa thought of one last Christmas present.

And from that day on,

Irwin was the boss.

Made in the USA
Charleston, SC
12 February 2015